MW01156326

# WHAT'S UNDER THE LOG?

By Anne Hunter

Houghton Mifflin Company
Boston

The text of this book is set in Goudy.
The illustrations are watercolor, colored pencil, and ink, reproduced in full color.

*Library of Congress Cataloging-in-Publication Data*

Hunter, Anne.
What's under the log? / Anne Hunter.
p.   cm.
Summary: Describes a variety of forest animals, including the red eft,
chipmunk, and ground beetle.
ISBN 0-395-75496-8
1. Forest animals—Ecology—Juvenile literature.  2. Forest animals—
Habitations—Juvenile literature.  [1. Forest animals.]  I. Title
QL112.H796    1999
591.73—dc21    98-49006  CIP  AC

Printed in Singapore
TWP 10 9 8 7 6 5 4

What's under the log?

# A Ground Beetle

The shiny, hard-shelled ground beetle lives under moist leaves and old logs. The ground beetle is a predator that hunts at night for caterpillars and soft-bodied insects. Although it generally travels by foot, the ground beetle has wings under the shiny shell on its back, which it can use to fly short distances. Ground beetles are about a half inch long.

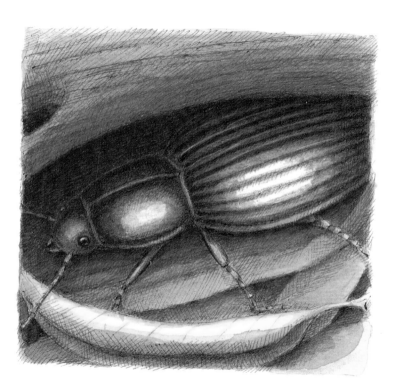

# A RED EFT

The red eft is a newt, which is a type of salamander that begins life underwater. It emerges to spend one to three years living on dry land, then returns to the water in later life to lay its eggs. In its land stage a newt is called an eft. Red efts are usually found in moist areas of the forest and live on a diet of worms and insects. The red eft is three to five inches in length.

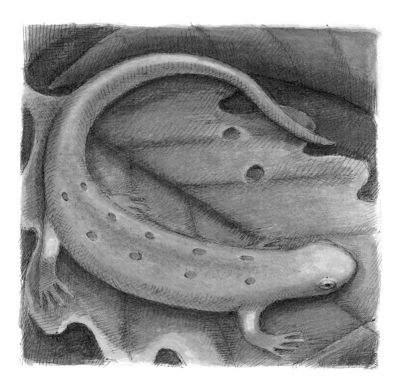

# A FIELD CRICKET

The field cricket lives under the log, where it is moist and protected from cool wind and weather. Field crickets feed on seeds, berries, and dead insects. On summer evenings they sing by scraping their wings over tiny filelike teeth on their backs. An adult field cricket is an inch long.

# A Sow Bug

The sow bug, also known as a wood louse, lives under the decaying wood of the log. Sow bugs have fourteen legs and their bodies are divided into many segments. The sow bug looks very much like its close relative the pill bug, which will roll into a ball when startled. An adult sow bug is about one third of an inch long.

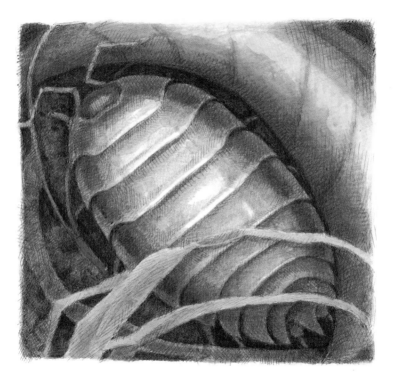

# A Chipmunk

The quick and industrious chipmunk hides under the log from such predators as hawks, owls, and foxes. Chipmunks eat seeds, nuts, fruit, and flower bulbs. They store food for the winter in underground tunnels, where they also hibernate. A chipmunk is eight to ten inches long from nose to tip of tail.

# A MILLIPEDE

*Millipede* is a Latin word that means a thousand feet. Millipedes don't actually have a thousand feet, but some kinds do have as many as seven hundred. The millipede's body is divided into many segments, each having a pair of legs. Millipedes feed on plants and often take shelter under old logs. They measure from one to five inches.

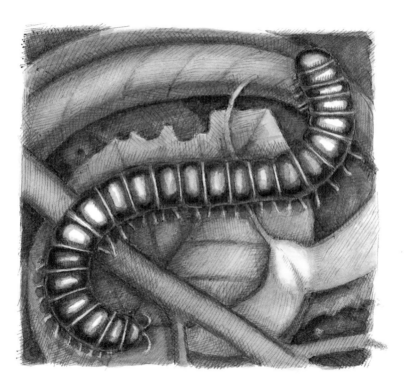

# A Velvet Mite

The tiny, brilliant red velvet mite is not much bigger than the head of a pin. Velvet mites have eight legs and are related to spiders. Their diet consists of small insects and insect eggs. Velvet mites are often found on old decaying wood.

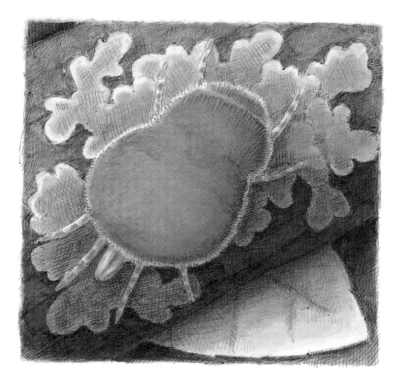

# A Daddy Longlegs

Daddy longlegs are also known as Harvestmen. These spiders do not weave webs but travel by foot in search of small insects and plant juices. When nights are cool, groups of the usually solitary daddy longlegs may be found gathered under logs with their legs entwined. Their legs may be as long as two inches.

# CARPENTER ANTS

The big black carpenter ants dig and live in tunnels in the decaying wood of the old log. They live in colonies, with many ants sharing a tunnel. Carpenter ants feed on insects, plant nectar, and anything containing sugar. They are a quarter to a half inch in length.

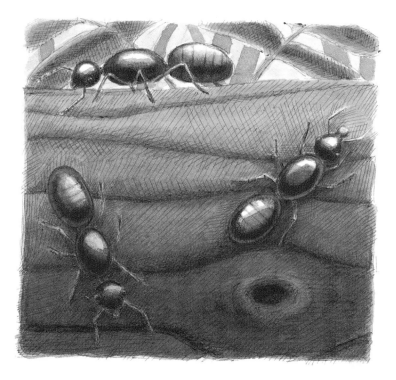

# A Garter Snake

The garter snake is camouflaged in the leaves and wood of the forest floor by its earthy-colored stripes. It often curls under the log for protection from predators or bad weather. Garter snakes feed on worms, frogs, insects, and salamanders. An adult garter snake may measure from one and a half to four feet.

A tree's life is not over when it falls down and becomes a log on the forest floor. Not only does the log provide a home and hiding place to many creatures (many more than are shown in this book), but as it decays the log returns important nutrients to the soil, which feed the new plants and trees that grow to replace the fallen tree.

Remember, if you look underneath a log, replace it carefully, since the log is home to so many creatures.